# Problems
## at the
# North Pole

# Problems at

# the North Pole

## written & illustrated by

## Lauren Peters

LANDMARK EDITIONS, INC.

P.O. Box 4469 • 1402 Kansas Avenue • Kansas City, Missouri 64127
(816) 241-4919

Dedicated to:

my parents, Marsha and Vic;
my sister, Lindsey;
and my grandparents,
"Marty" and "Pawpaw" Kimberlin.
Without the support of my loving family,
this book would never have happened.

Second Printing

COPYRIGHT © 1990 BY LAUREN PETERS

International Standard Book Number: 0-933849-25-7 (LIB.BDG.)

Library of Congress Cataloging-in-Publication Data
Peters, Lauren, 1981-
    Problems at the North Pole / written and illustrated by Lauren Peters.
    p.      cm.
    Summary: Santa's decision to take a winter vacation creates chaos at the North
Pole and endangers Christmas.
    ISBN 0-933849-25-7 (lib.bdg.)
    1. Santa Claus — Juvenile fiction. [1. Santa Claus — Fiction.
    2. Christmas — Fiction.]
I. Title.
PZ7.P44163Pr          1990          [E] — dc20          90-5929
                                                        CIP
                                                        AC

Editorial Coordinator: Nancy R. Thatch
Creative Coordinator: David Melton

Printed in the United States of America

Landmark Editions, Inc.
P.O. Box 4469
1402 Kansas Avenue
Kansas City, Missouri 64127
(816) 241-4919

# PROBLEMS AT THE NORTH POLE

The purpose of The National Written & Illustrated by... Contest is to search nationwide and find exceptionally talented young authors and illustrators. Surely, there is some irony in finding a young creator who lives less then twenty miles from our offices. But that's exactly what happened when Lauren Peters' book, PROBLEMS AT THE NORTH POLE, became a winner in the 1989 Contest.

When winning students live hundreds of miles away, our staff members must coordinate preparations of their final manuscripts and illustrations by mail and long distance telephone conferences. But since Lauren lived nearby, we enjoyed the privilege of working with her in person as she prepared her book for publication.

Our staff loved watching Lauren paint her illustrations! Her sense of color and line is extraordinary, and her feeling for composition and point of view is years beyond her age. As she refined her illustrations, it was also exciting for us to see the vast improvements in her drawing skills. Her parents were astounded!

Lauren charmed everyone at Landmark. She was polite, outgoing, and full of exuberance. She also knew the proper way to treat a publisher — one day she brought Christmas cookies to us.

Both children and adults should be filled with good cheer as they read her delightful book.

— David Melton
Creative Coordinator
Landmark Editions, Inc.

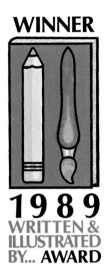

WINNER

**1989**
WRITTEN &
ILLUSTRATED
BY... AWARD

After Santa Claus delivers all the presents on Christmas Eve, he returns to the North Pole to celebrate. On Christmas Day he and Mrs. Claus, the Elves, and the reindeer open their gifts. Then they relax and enjoy a delicious lunch.

For dessert Mrs. Claus prepares her special plum pie — Santa's favorite dish. She knows he is sure to take a second slice, or even a third. So Mrs. Claus bakes plum pie only on Christmas because Santa does have a bit of a weight problem.

The day after Christmas, everyone at the North Pole returns to work. They must begin to prepare for the next Christmas.

Mrs. Claus checks her supplies for making candy canes and baking cookies.

"Let me see," she says. "I'll need 10,000 tons of flour, 30,000 tons of sugar, 300 gallons of vanilla, 600 pounds of cinnamon and 200 truckloads of chocolate chips."

The Elves sweep the workshop and sharpen their woodcarving tools. They order thousands of needles, miles of thread, stuffing for dolls, wheels for bicycles, blocks of wood, and gallons of paint in every color.

The reindeer jog around the track and practice leaping high into the air. They know they must keep in perfect shape for their once-a-year trip.

At his office Santa reads the mail and updates the list of children's names. Some people think that Santa still writes his list by hand. But he no longer does that. His secretary, Ms. Bumby, now enters all information into a new computer.

And no matter what the popular song says, Santa doesn't have to check his list twice. The computer has a super spellcheck and a speedy zip code finder.

Everyone at the North Pole works very hard all year long. They know how important it is to have everything ready by the next Christmas Eve. This is the way it has always been…that is, until last year.

Last year something terrible happened!

The problem began on a cold, cold morning in late November. As Santa was reading his mail, he discovered a colorful folder, that read:

Escape from the Cold! Fly to Hawaii for Half Price!

Santa always liked to find a good bargain. And he loved sandy beaches and sunny skies. He could almost feel the warm sunlight on his face and hear the ocean waves splash against the shore.

Suddenly a blast of cold arctic wind hit against the window and made Santa shiver. Right then and there, he decided he had to go to Hawaii. Without telling anyone, he wrote a check and mailed it that very day.

Mrs. Claus soon noticed that Santa had something on his mind. Each day when she said, "Good morning, Santa," he would smile and reply, "Aloha!"

The Elves also noticed that Santa was acting strangely. Several times a day, they saw him suddenly start to wiggle back and forth. They wondered if Santa was shivering from the cold or if he was trying to do a hula dance.

Even Ms. Bumby noticed Santa's strange behavior. Before she could open the mail each morning, he would rush in and rummage through the stacks. He seemed to be looking for a special letter.

Before long that special letter arrived. Santa ripped open the envelope and looked inside. Then he yelled, "Ho! Ho! Ho!", and ran straight to the house.

"The tickets are here!" he shouted, holding them out. "Get ready, Mrs. Claus! We are going to Hawaii for a vacation!"

"Have you lost your mind!" she exclaimed. "We can't take a vacation. There's too much work to be done."

And then something happened that had never happened before — Mr. and Mrs. Claus got into an argument!

Minutes later Santa stomped out of the house, carrying his suitcase.

"Then I'll go to Hawaii without you!" he announced stubbornly.

And that's exactly what Santa did. He jumped onto his jet-propelled skis, and with a puff of smoke, he headed across the snow toward the airport.

The Elves, Ms. Bumby, and the reindeer didn't know what to do. So they just kept on working.

When Santa got off the airplane in Hawaii, girls in hula skirts slipped flowered leis around his neck. And they greeted him with the one word he wanted to hear — "ALOHA!"

16

During his vacation Santa enjoyed sunning himself on the beach and swimming in the ocean. He even learned to ride a surfboard. And Santa didn't worry about a thing. He was sure that Mrs. Claus, Ms. Bumby, and all the Elves and reindeer were busy getting everything ready for Christmas.

But back at the North Pole, things were not going as Santa supposed.

After Santa had left, Mrs. Claus did not come out of the house. She even stopped baking cookies for the Elves' morning coffee breaks. The Elves began to worry about her. After a few days, one of them tiptoed to the house and peeked through a window. He could hardly believe what he saw.

There sat Mrs. Claus in a comfortable chair. She was wearing a swimming suit, sipping lemonade, and reading a book.

When the other Elves heard that Mrs. Claus wasn't working, they decided they would not work either.

Instead, they played video games all day long. And at night they stayed up late, playing dominoes and eating popcorn.

When Ms. Bumby saw no one else was working, she stopped opening the mail. All she did was watch her favorite soap operas on television.

When the reindeer found out that Mrs. Claus, the Elves, and Ms. Bumby were not working, they stopped doing their daily exercises. Instead of running and leaping, they listened to music and munched on cinnamon cookies. They grew lazier and fatter by the day.

If Santa had known that all work at the North Pole had come to a complete stop, he would have taken the next airplane home. But Santa did not know.

When his two-week vacation ended, Santa flew home on Arctic Airlines. He was eager to see the new toys the Elves had made. And he hoped Mrs. Claus had forgotten all about their argument. Perhaps she had even baked some extra cookies just for him.

As he skied away from the airport, he felt a sudden rush of the Christmas spirit. He sang, "Jingle Bells," all the way home.

But when he reached the North Pole, he was surprised to find that no one was working. The reindeer were not running on the track. The Elves were not carrying boxes to the warehouse. And he didn't smell cookies baking either.

"What's going on here?" he demanded to know as he entered his house.

"Oh, you're back," Mrs. Claus replied calmly as she dried her fingernails. "Did you have a nice time on your vacation, Dear?"

"Why isn't everyone working?" he asked excitedly.

"We decided to take a vacation too," she replied sweetly.

Santa's tanned face turned a deep red, and he walked straight to his office. Mail was stacked high in every corner. Ms. Bumbly, of course, was not at the computer. She had gone home early.

For a long time, Santa sat at his desk and thought about the problems he had caused. He knew he had no one to blame but himself.

The next morning Santa called a meeting.

"Christmas is only two weeks away," he said sadly. "I don't think we can finish all the presents in time. We'll just have to announce that there will be NO CHRISTMAS this year."

"We can't do that!" Mrs. Claus exclaimed. "Just think how disappointed the children will be."

"I know," Santa sighed. "But what can we do?"

"I'm willing to work overtime," Ms. Bumby offered.

"We'll work double shifts," the Elves volunteered.

"I'll heat up the extra ovens," Mrs. Claus said.

And the reindeer stretched their legs and began doing kneebends.

"Okay," Santa agreed. "If we work day and night, perhaps we can save Christmas after all."

So everyone set to work immediately.

The Elves hurried to the workshop and started the toy-making machines.

Mrs. Claus lit all of the ovens and mixed up huge batches of cookie dough.

The reindeer jogged, jumped and leaped. They took turns bouncing on the trampoline. And they did aerobic dancing to shake off the extra pounds they had gained.

Ms. Bumby quickly opened the mail and began adding more children's names to Santa's list.

Santa was busy too. He helped the Elves make the toys.

He helped Mrs. Claus decorate cookies and stripe the candy canes.

He rubbed the reindeer's sore muscles with liniment and turned on the Jacuzzi.

And he helped Ms. Bumby check the computer printouts.

By working day and night, the Elves finished all of the toys by Christmas Eve. Mrs. Claus filled her pantry with mounds of goodies to stuff in children's stockings. Ms. Bumby completed the list of names. And the reindeer were in perfect shape and ready to make their long journey.

But there was one more problem. When Santa put on his red suit, it didn't fit!

"Oh, no!" Mrs. Claus gasped. "You lost too much weight while you were in Hawaii. Now your suit is too big!"

Thinking quickly, she handed Santa a pair of suspenders and told him to fasten them to his trousers. Then she stuffed pillows under his jacket.

"You're thin enough to eat all the plum pie you want this year," she said with a smile.

"I'll do just that," Santa laughed, and he and Mrs. Claus hurried outside.

Everyone cheered as Santa climbed into his sleigh. He cracked his whip and yelled, "On Dancer! On Cupid! On Donder and Blitzen, and all the rest of you! We're off!"

Proudly wearing their new Reeboks, the reindeer scattered the snow as they raced across the ground. Then with a mighty leap, they sprang into the air, taking Santa and his sleigh full of toys over the treetops and into the starry night.

You can be sure that no one at the North Pole will ever forget the year they almost missed Christmas.

And Santa has promised that he will never again take a vacation during the winter. But to make certain that Santa keeps his promise, Mrs. Claus has given special instructions to his secretary. Each morning Ms. Bumby is to remove all vacation folders before Santa sees the mail.

# THE NATIONAL WRITTEN & ILLUSTRATED

## — THE 1989 NATIONAL AWARD WINNING BOOKS —

**Lauren Peters**
age 7

**Michael Cain**
age 11

Problems at the North Pole

Written & Illustrated by Lauren Peters

the Legend of SIR MIGUEL

MICHAEL CAIN

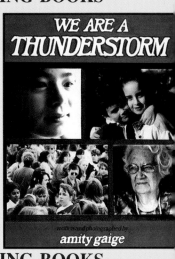

WE ARE A THUNDERSTORM

written and photographed by amity gaige

## —THE 1987 NATIONAL AWARD WINNING BOOKS—

**Amity Gaige**
age 16

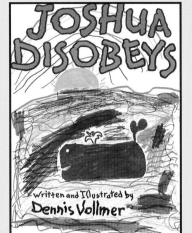

JOSHUA DISOBEYS

Written and Illustrated by Dennis Vollmer

THE HALF & HALF DOG

written and illustrated by LISA GROSS

who owns the sun?

~written & illustrated by~ STACY CHBOSKY

## —THE 1989 GOLD AWARD WINNERS—

BROKEN ARROW BOY

WRITTEN AND ILLUSTRATED BY ADAM MOORE and his friends

GET THAT GOAT!

WRITTEN AND ILLUSTRATED BY MICHAEL AUSHENKER

### Students' Winning Books
### Motivate and Inspire

Each year it is Landmark's pleasure to publish the winning books The National Written & Illustrate By... Awards Contest For Student These are important books because the supply such positive motivation a inspiration for other talented studen to write and illustrate books too!

### Students of All Ages
### Love the Winning Books

Students of all ages enjoy readir these fascinating books created by o young author/illustrators. When st dents see the beautiful books, print in full color and handsomely bound hardback covers, they, too, will be come excited about writing and illu trating books and eager to enter the in the Contest.

### Enter Your Book
### In the Next Contest

If you are 6 to 19 years of ag you may enter the Contest too. Pe haps your book may be one of the ne winners and you will become a pu lished author and illustrator too.

**Stacy Chbosky**
age 14

**Adam Moore**
age 9

**Michael Aushenker**
age 19

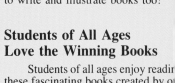
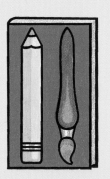
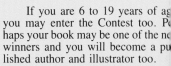